# Ollie

## Olivier Dunrea

WALKER BOOKS
AND SUBSIDIARIES

LONDON · BOSTON · SYDNEY · AUCKLAND

First published in Great Britain 2004 by Walker Books Ltd
87 Vauxhall Walk, London SE11 5HJ

This edition published 2006

2 4 6 8 10 9 7 5 3 1

© 2003 Olivier Dunrea
Published by arrangement with Houghton Mifflin Company

This book has been typeset in Shannon

Printed in China

British Library Cataloguing in Publication Data:
a catalogue record for this book is available from the British Library

ISBN-13: 978-1-4063-0120-5
ISBN-10: 1-4063-0120-5

www.walkerbooks.co.uk

*For Wayne*

This is Ollie.

Ollie is waiting.

He won't come out.

Gossie and Gertie have been waiting
for weeks for Ollie to come out.

"I won't come out," says Ollie.

He rolls to the left.

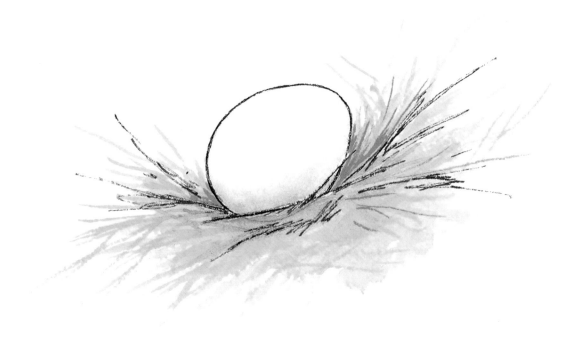

He rolls to the right.

He stands on his head.

He hides in the straw.
He won't come out.

Gossie pokes Ollie with her bill.

Gertie listens to Ollie with her ear.

"I won't come out!" says Ollie.

He holds his breath.

He rolls out of the nest.

He rolls over the stones.

He rolls under the sheep.
He won't come out.

Gossie runs after Ollie.

Gertie runs after Ollie.

"I won't come out!" says Ollie.

Gossie and Gertie sit on top of Ollie.

"Don't come out," says Gossie.

"Don't come out," says Gertie.

Ollie waits.

Then he begins cracking!

"I'm out!" he says.